Sam the Very Shy Snail

...my friend you're never alone. ♡

love Sam

Written and illustrated by: Peter Jarvis

JARVIS '19

This book belongs to:

— — — — — — — — — — — — — — — — — —

Whose friends are:

— — — — — — — — — — — — — — — — — —

— — — — — — — — — — — — — — — — — —

— — — — — — — — — — — — — — — — — —

— — — — — — — — — — — — — — — — — —

The Salty Garden / Stop Bugging Me Books brings you:
Sam the very shy snail

First published in 2019
Text & Illustrations copyright © 2019 Peter Jarvis

A CIP record for this book is available from the British Library upon request.

ISBN: 9781696397780

This book is dedicated to all of those people who were there for me when I needed them the most.

Thank you for your love, support, kindness, generosity and care.

You have taught me the true meaning of friendship.

I love you all.

Every Monday,
Monty the mole
would shuffle from
his homely hole.

He would wriggle
his snout and
whiff up the air.

Move a mountain
of mud without
a care.

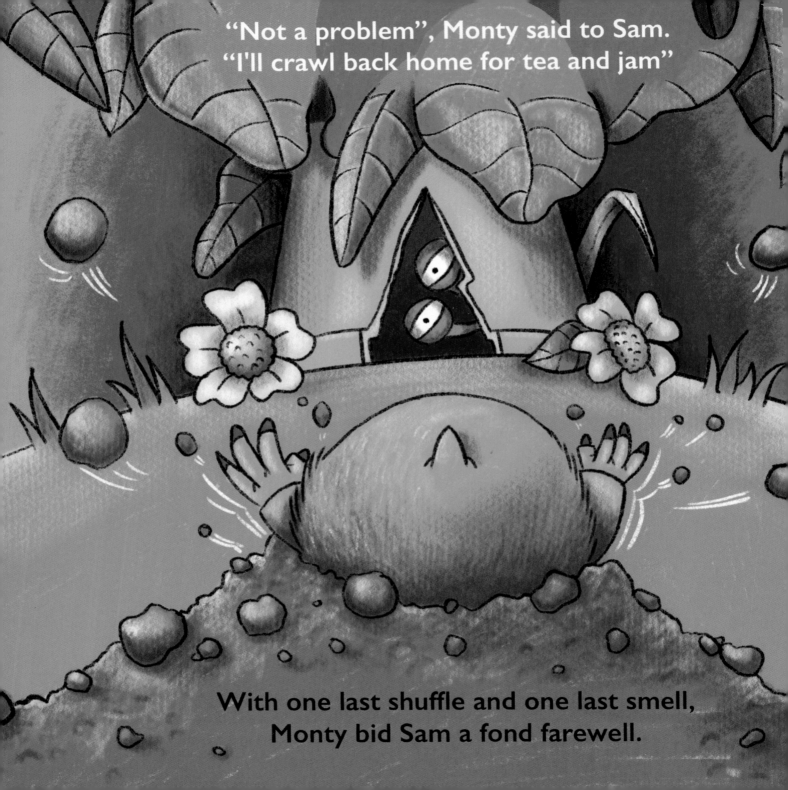

Every Tuesday, Bayley the Bee
would buzz down from the very tall tree.

He'd bob and buzz in the air for a while,
in a fancy loop-the-loop stunt-bee style.

"No problem Sam", Bayley said
buzzing back home.
"Today, I don't mind if I play
on my own"

With one last bumble
and a loop-the-loop,
he flew out of sight
with a whoosh and a swoop.

Every
Wednesday
Winnie
the worm...

...would appear from the ground
with a wiggle and a squirm.

She'd wriggle along the soft muddy ground,
sneak up on Sam without making a sound.

"Sam will you come out
and say howdy-doo?,
I hope I didn't frighten you!

"Not a problem Sam".
Winnie said to her friend.
"I'll slink back home
so you can mend"

With one wiggly wriggle
and one slickly slither,
Winnie slipped away
without a dither.

Every Thursday a toad named Tom
would hop and bounce across the pond.

With a hippidy, hoppidy, huppidy, hop ...

With one last ...

JUMP

... a

HOP

... and a

SKIP

Tom bounced away with a Toodle-pip.

Every Friday, Filby the fly
would flip and fall
from up in the sky.

He'd fancifully flap his small flappy wings
and clumsily collide with big garden things.

Sam would ponder and
then reply,
"Filby I can't, I'm just too shy!"

"No problem, flapped Filby,
I'll be on my way.
We can sing a new song
some other fine day"

With a flappity,
flabbidy,
flippidy,
flip....

...Filby flew
away swiftly
without a blip.

Every Saturday,
Spencer the spider
sailed from the shed
like a spidery glider.

Spinning his web
at a such silly speeds,
he'd land like a stunt bug
into the weeds.

"Sam it's Spencer, join me in the sun.
We can spin my webs, it's so much fun"

Sam would ponder
and then reply,
"Spencer I can't,
I'm just too shy!"

"It's not a problem Sam",
Spencer cried.
"It is rather hot,
you should stay inside"

With one last shot of his silky soft web,
Spencer spun back to his web on the shed.

"What a wonderful day", he'd say full of glee.
"I don't have to spin webs, dig holes or climb trees"

"But I do wish my friends
were around here to play.
I'd love to be silly
and not shy for one day"

really early in the morning,
Sam appeared
stretching and yawning.

What Sam didn't know
was all of his friends,
were watching him play
through a big hole in the fence.

"He'll play out when he's ready", Filby quietly said.

Spencer agreed, as he Spun a new web.

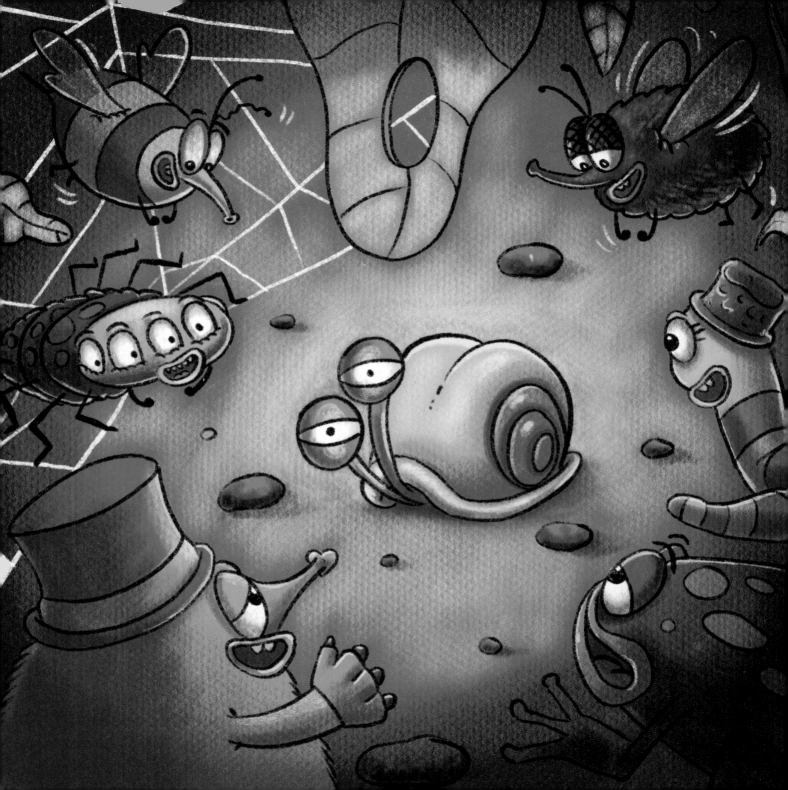

They knew Sam liked time on his own.
They are there when he needs them ...
he's never alone.

Use all of your friends favourite colours
to add some colour to Sams friends lives.

Use the following pages to draw
your friends or your favourite garden bugs.